One Drop of Kindness

Written by: Jeff Kubiak

Illustrated by: Liliana Mora

The sign read "The Kindness Academy of World Changing Students." By the looks of it, you could sense it was a glorious and magical place of learning. Yes, this was THE school to be in! It had everything that a child could imagine — play, mindfulness, coding, cooking, welding, STEAM, student choice, and of course, no homework! But it wasn't always like this...

It was an unsettled start for the messy, long-haired, freckled Gus. A few years after he was born, Gus's mother passed away and he was moved from home to home, and school to school, sometimes staying only a day or two. Many of these places were dilapidated and run down, and at times, you could hear nothing but an eerie silence. But a whisper from his loving mother would stay with him always,

"One drop of Kindness is all it takes to fill a heart with Love."

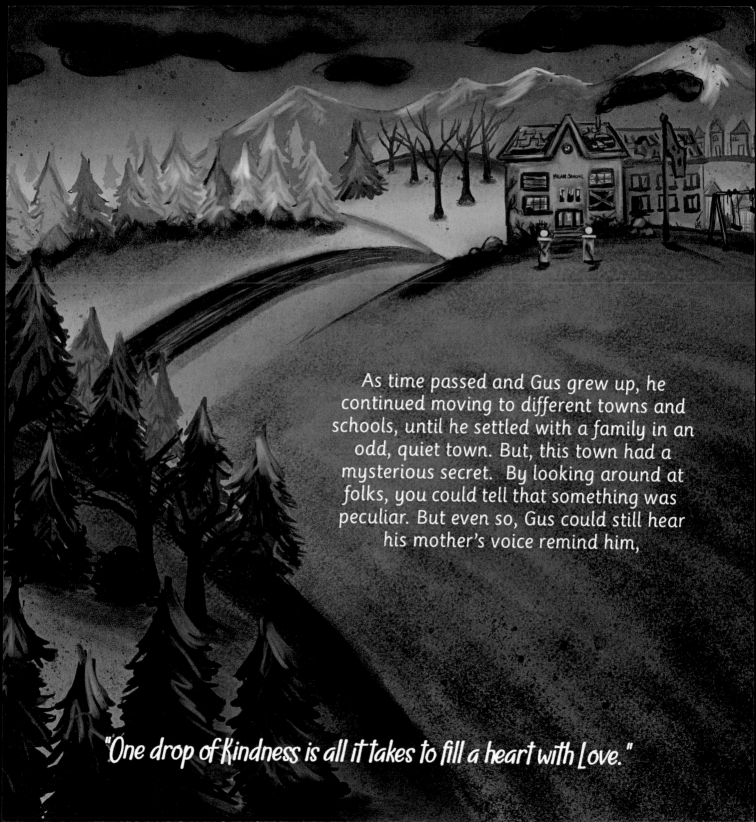

As time passed and Gus grew up, he continued moving to different towns and schools, until he settled with a family in an odd, quiet town. But, this town had a mysterious secret. By looking around at folks, you could tell that something was peculiar. But even so, Gus could still hear his mother's voice remind him,

"One drop of Kindness is all it takes to fill a heart with Love."

Gus attended a school called Midvale Elementary at Northpark, nicknamed the "MEAN School." This place was heartless. You could tell by the looks, gestures, and cringy body language from people that this was not a kind community. This was part of the town's puzzling secret.

"One drop of Kindness is all it takes to fill a heart with Love," whispered in the wind.

Gus was noticeable the moment he entered school for the first time. He had a grim look, furrowed brow, and was glum. Students and teachers would avoid him or cringe as he passed. You see, Gus was sad and heartbroken. No one had taken the time to learn his story.

"One drop of Kindness is all it takes to fill a heart with Love," echoed his mother's voice.

It became normal to be uncaring here. People were sad, dejected, and insensitive. Frowns, snarls, and tears were common at MEAN School. Little did people know the one ingredient that could break this way of life was just One Drop of Kindness. But Gus hadn't found it yet. He continued to scowl and make life miserable for others, even though he could always hear,

"One drop of Kindness is all it takes to fill a heart with Love,"

somewhere in his mind.

There were no signs of kindness anywhere at MEAN School. Imagine that!
Words, actions, and gestures were hurtful, and even upsetting at times.
No one knew how to behave any different. Looking around the dirty, dingy,
and dilapidated school that had a sour, mushroomy odor to it,
one could sense the sadness.

"One drop of Kindness is all it takes to fill a heart with Love."

Recess at school was a mess. There was no sharing during games: balls were weapon-like, and play equipment was destroyed and broken. Gus was the King of recess mischief. He was the leader of arguing, teasing, and not taking turns. Teachers yelled at almost everyone, and worst of all, students would say uncaring words and mean it! Despite all the sadness, these words still rang in Gus's ear,

"One drop of Kindness is all it takes to fill a heart with Love."

Classrooms at MEAN School were no different. They were filled with teachers reprimanding children. Students were made to clean whiteboards and pencil sharpeners, and scrub the floors and desks. There wasn't a smile to be found, especially on Gus. Kindness was NOWHERE to be seen or heard.

"One drop of Kindness is all it takes to fill a heart with Love."

Slowly, students stopped coming to MEAN School. At times, half of them wouldn't show up! Gus didn't care. He had no one at home that noticed, so he thought causing trouble at school was what he was meant to do. You see, no one had yet discovered the powers that kindness could bring.

"One drop of Kindness is all it takes to fill a heart with Love."

This pattern of sadness, sorrow, and school-wide misery grew, because the despair became overpowering. People acted like zombies, not fully realizing what they were doing. Gus's heart shrank even smaller, like a shriveled prune, as he was overcome with emptiness, dejection, and loss.

"One drop of Kindness is all it takes to fill a heart with Love," whirled around Gus, then settled deep inside.

One blustery fall day, something extraordinary
happened! A new girl entered MEAN School.
A gleeful girl. A kind girl. A bubbly girl. A girl that
laughed, smiled, and genuinely cared about others!
A girl with a heart so big, it rivaled a blue whale's!
The girl's name was Truly. And suddenly, a whisper
filled the air,

"One drop of Kindness is all it takes to fill a heart with Love."

Truly was angelic, with stunning dark eyes. Her feather-like hair almost floated behind her like a superhero's cape. Truly beamed as she stepped into the classroom. The teacher and students were astounded! The first words out of Truly's mouth were, "What a lovely school!" Gus stood in shock. His mouth gaped open, and the furrowed brow began to disappear. Grins slowly filled the classroom, hearts began to grow, and hope trickled into their minds. Then they all heard a hum:

"One drop of Kindness is all it takes to fill a heart with Love."

Truly's impact was transforming. It became the most incredible ripple effect of KINDNESS ever felt! If there was one student who stood out as the most inspired, it was Gus. This once-abandoned boy blossomed the day Truly drifted into his classroom.

"One drop of Kindness is all it takes to fill a heart with Love."

The metamorphosis at MEAN School was sensational. Gus's embrace with kindness had the whole school talking. Gus began spearheading changes that he and Truly wanted to bring about at MEAN school. Everyone began to call him "Gus, The Kindness Kid," and he took on this new role with heartfelt love! He finally began to understand the sweet echo that had been with him since he was a baby —

"One drop of Kindness is all it takes to fill a heart with Love."

Over the next few weeks, the school became eye-poppingly gorgeous! Graffiti was painted over. Smiles were everywhere. Teachers and students began to connect and build relationships, coming together like peanut butter and jelly. Parents were seen volunteering to read with students, rebuilding the garden, and participating in Random Acts of Kindness ! Gus's heart overflowed, as he was so elated by this new energy the community began to share.

"One drop of Kindness is all it takes to fill a heart with Love."

The newly formed #RandomActsOfKindness Club became a wave of awesomeness at school! Their first mission? To rename MEAN school to something more fitting. Amazing ideas were offered, but everyone agreed that one name stood above all: "The Kindness Academy of World-Changing Students."

MIDVALE ELEMENTARY AT NORTHWAY

The Kindness Academy
of World Changing Students

"One drop of Kindness is all it takes to fill a heart with Love."

With the new school name came a huge amount of pride — throughout the community. School attendance quickly grew to 100%. After all, who wanted to miss a day of school? Children would run in the school doors long before the first bell rang! Classes practiced mindfulness, and teachers led with love. Gus showed others how to share and care. If there were disagreements, students would find kind ways to solve problems.

"One drop of Kindness is all it takes to fill a heart with Love."

The Kindness Academy quickly became known throughout the world as THE model for all schools. Gus and Truly were over the moon with joy! They talked about how everyone has the capacity of kindness and should all be "Kindness Ambassadors."

"This may be just what the world needs!" thought Truly, beaming with excitement.

"One drop of Kindness is all it takes to fill a heart with Love."

Schools near and far began to follow the Kindness Academy's model. Quickly, this kindness movement became a worldwide phenomenon. The leaders of countries even took an oath, vowing to lead with passion and let kindness help inform their decisions. Gus's name became known around the world, and people everywhere wanted to be like "Gus, the Kindness Kid."

"One drop of Kindness is all it takes to fill a heart with Love."

Strangely, one day Gus felt sad and lonely, so he headed to the office to ask if anyone had seen Truly. The school's Principal, Ms. Friendly sounded puzzled, "Truly?" she asked. "Yes, Ms. Friendly," replied Gus, "I can't find her. Truly is the sole reason that our school is so amazing now!" Ms. Friendly paused for a moment, took Gus by the hand, and walked him into her office.

"One drop of Kindness is all it takes to fill a heart with Love,"

she whispered into his ear.

Holding back tears, Gus stammered, "Truly brought kindness to our school and community. She was my best friend and the Queen of Random Acts of Kindness."

"Sweet Gus, it is YOU who is our Kindness Ambassador. It has always been in your heart, your soul, and in everything you do. You carry love, compassion, and kindness within you. Truly just helped to bring it out in you. Remember Gus, *One drop of Kindness is all it takes to fill a heart with Love,"*

she said.

Ms. Friendly continued with a tear in her eye and a crackle in her voice. "Gus, you ARE Truly, she's in YOUR heart. Everyone has kindness within them Gus, but some people need to dig deeper to find it. Now that we know the way of kindness, it will never fade. Gus, you truly are The Kindness Kid to all now. Never forget.

One drop of Kindness is all it takes to fill a heart with Love."

"Use your courage Gus, to change the world," she said, after a hug and a smile. This school, the town, and their world had become a much better place for everyone to live and belong. Gus smiled, thinking how he was a part of a kind family at school and home. This once-desolate town with a secret found that all along, they just needed "One Drop of Kindness."

Activities and Discussion Ideas

• What is **Kindness** to you?
• Will you perform 3 Acts of **Kindness** this week?
• What is 1 thing you can do to spread **Kindness** today?
• What can you do to stand up to bullies without hurting back?
• What is an activity that can be done with friends or family that spreads **Kindness**?
• Cut out 4 **Kindness** cards and share them with friends.
• Sometimes we have bad days and just don't feel kind. What is something you can do to share **Kindness** with someone who is having a bad day?
• How can you help make school a more kind place for all kids, so that they want to run back each and every day?
• Just like Gus transformed MEAN School with **Kindness**, what are 3 things you could do today to help improve the community at YOUR School?
• Do you know someone that might be sad, or heartbroken, or even almost "invisible?" Please pass on some **Kindness** to help him/her smile, feel noticed, and happy!
• Does your school have a RAK (Random Acts of **Kindness**) Club? If not, why not talk to your teachers or parents and try to start one? You could paint **Kindness** sayings on rocks and hide them. Or, every Wednesday, share some **Kindness** notes, do campus beautification, or ask everyone to share at least 1 act of **Kindness**!
What a ripple effect that would be!

If you do have a RAK Club, share your great ideas with me on
Twitter @jeffreykubiak and Hashtag #OneDropOfKindness.
Or go to jeffkubiak.com and share!

About the Author

Jeff Kubiak is the principal of Nelda Mundy Elementary School with over 18 years of school service. Jeff taught for eleven years as an elementary school teacher and has seven years of administrative experience. He strives to connect with ALL students by bringing real-world experiences to them, getting to know their names, engaging in lessons and play, and becoming a part of the learning process with them. Jeff has always looked at education from a different lens: from someone who hated school and struggled with a "one size fits all" system. He vowed that he would always do his best to increase opportunities for all students to feel heard, noticed, celebrated, challenged, and safe. Jeff works hard to push back against the old model of "Industrialized Education" and fights conformity. There is not a day that goes by that he is not looking ahead to improve teacher pedagogy, student engagement and digital access for all. Jeff is a former world-class swimmer and coach, and looks at education from perspectives that others don't. He knows what it takes to fail, struggle, and go through the daily challenges that we all might face. Jeff has a vision of #KidsFirst thinking, student voice, All Kids Can, and a kindness focused culture. Jeff is based in California, is married to his wife, Piper, and father to Keeley and Braden. He can be found at jeffkubiak.com, on Twitter at @jeffreykubiak and blog at principalkubiak.blogspot.com.

This book would not have been possible without the love from my sixth grade teacher, Mrs. Paula Sherry. She was the one who helped make education a positive experience for me. She was thoughtful, brilliant, had high expectations, and most importantly, she believed in me. Mrs. Sherry also showed me the way of Kindness. I am forever grateful for you Mrs. Sherry, you are truly missed.

Acknowledgements

I am so grateful to my amazing wife, Piper Andersen Kubiak for her endless support and tremendous heart, my parents Robert and Melissa Kubiak, my sister Marian and my two lovely children; Keeley and Braden.

I'm so blessed to know Kindness Educators such as Roman Nowak, Tamara Letter, Laurie McIntosh, Kristen Nan, Adam Welcome, Kas Nelson, and many others. I love following and learning from the great Brad Montague — creator of Kid President. Also, thank you to Ellen DeGeneres, Michael Franti, Rich Roll, Rachel Joy Scott, Oprah Winfrey, Jon Gordon, Ghandi and so many others for the positive and kind messages to the world. I'm blessed for my amazing Focus Group and most importantly to the amazing Liliana Mora for her epic art and illustrations and bringing Gus to life!

Of course, this book would not have been possible without Mandy Froehlich, who introduced me to Sarah Thomas of EduMatch Publishing. These two believed in me and my message of One Drop Of Kindness!

And finally, to all of my #PLN friends who read, reflected, and helped me bring this book to life!

One Drop Of Kindness
By Jeff Kubiak
Published by EduMatch®
PO Box 150324, Alexandria, VA 22315

Note from the author: A portion of the book proceeds will help spread kindness to our world. We'll donate items such as: safe/clean drinking water, shoes, socks, blankets or beanies to schools and communities in need. Also, to purchase copies of One Drop of Kindness for schools in need, as I believe all schools should share the kindness message that Gus brings to us.

www.edumatchpublishing.com

ISBN-13: 978-1-970133-08-0
ISBN-10: 1-970133-08-2

"One Drop Of Kindness is truly a game changing book! Jeff Kubiak tells the story of transformation, kindness, and the power each and every child and person has to change the culture and those around them.
Resonate kindness and others around you will as well!"
— Adam Welcome, Educator, Speaker,
Author of #KidsDeserveIt & Run Like a Pirate

"This book should be read in every school in every classroom. There is so much negativity in the world that if everyone took One Drop of Kindness to heart it would be a much better place."— Cate Rockstad, EdD. Stockton Unified School District

"Jeff has taken his life's work and created a way for others to learn from his leadership. The story of Gus is relatable for all of us and a great reminder that do be able to do great things, it starts with one small act of kindness."
— Jessica Cabeen, 2017 Nationally Distinguished Principal,
Author of Hacking Early Learning, co-author of Balance Like a Pirate,
and national speaker.

"One Drop of Kindness reminds us our vibes are contagious, that all it takes is one person to start a ripple effect, and that we can change one another's lives! This book is perfect for home, classrooms, and staff meetings. Share it and start your own ripple today!"
— Sarah Johnson, co-author of Balance Like a Pirate

One Drop of Kindness

Kindness Cards

Give one when you see the need.

Spreading kindness creates a ripple effect.

Give someone a Smile!

You are ultra-awesome!

I smile when I see you!

You make the world better!

Give 3 people compliments today

Here is a hug from me to you!

I will do a favor for you today

Help someone before they ask

Here's a high 5 for being awesome!

Made in the USA
San Bernardino, CA
17 May 2019